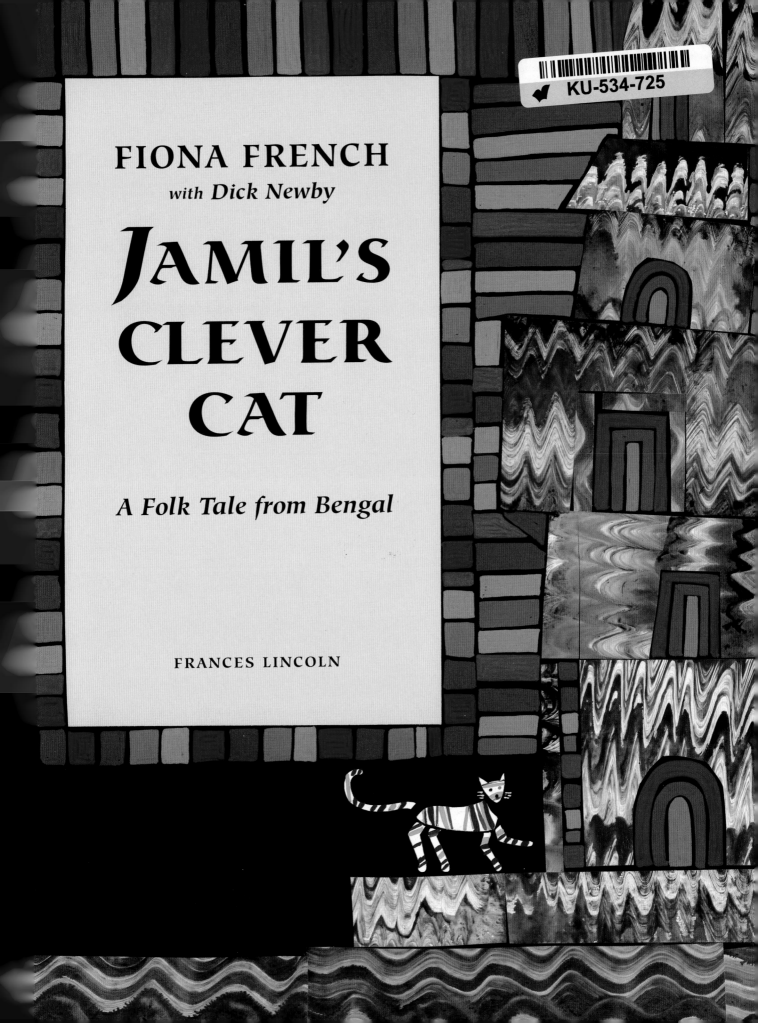

FIONA FRENCH
with *Dick Newby*

JAMIL'S CLEVER CAT

A Folk Tale from Bengal

FRANCES LINCOLN

Jamil the weaver lived
on the poor side of town.
He had a cat called
Sardul, a very clever cat.
Each night, while Jamil
was asleep, Sardul wove
material for his master to
make into tunics and saris.

One morning, Jamil sighed, and said, "Oh Sardul, if only I could marry the princess who lives in the palace! Then you and I would not have to work our fingers and paws to the bone, and I would be a very happy man."

Sardul thought for a minute. Then he said, "Give me the best waistcoat and the most beautiful sari we have made, Master, and I will make your dream come true."

Sardul leapt silently over the roofs of the city, carrying the sari and waistcoat on his back. Looking down, he saw the princess in the palace garden.

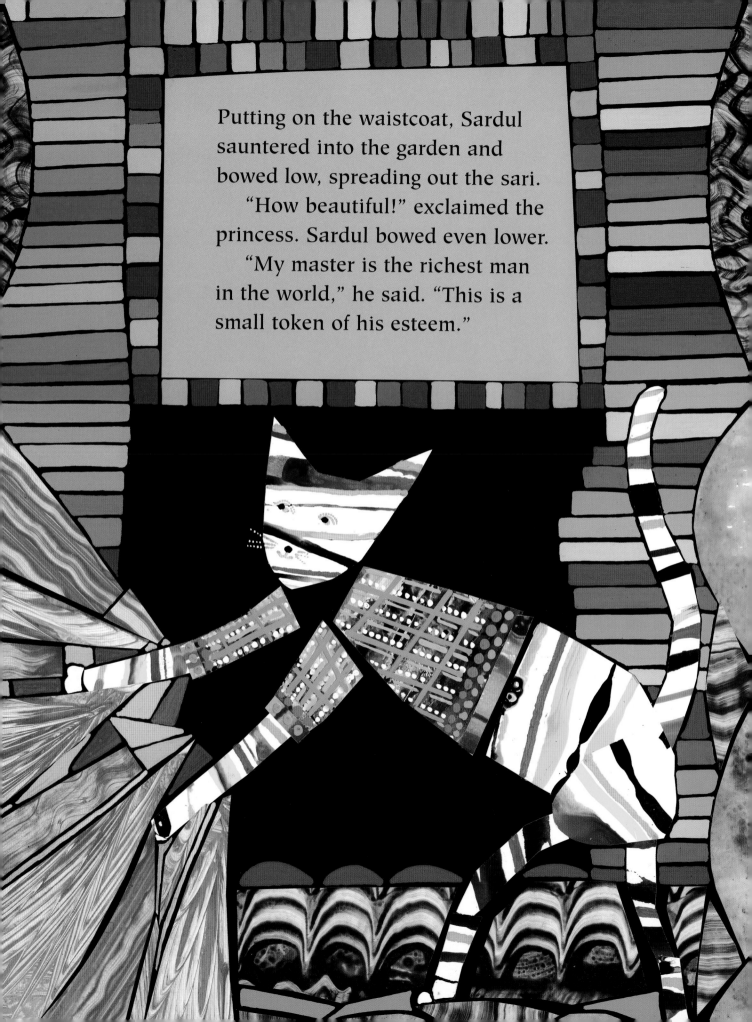

Putting on the waistcoat, Sardul
sauntered into the garden and
bowed low, spreading out the sari.

"How beautiful!" exclaimed the
princess. Sardul bowed even lower.

"My master is the richest man
in the world," he said. "This is a
small token of his esteem."

The princess was
so flattered, she took
Sardul to meet her parents.
"Such a generous gift!" said
the Rajah. "Would your master
like to marry our daughter?"

"I think she would do very nicely," answered Sardul, and taking his leave, he went back to Jamil the weaver.

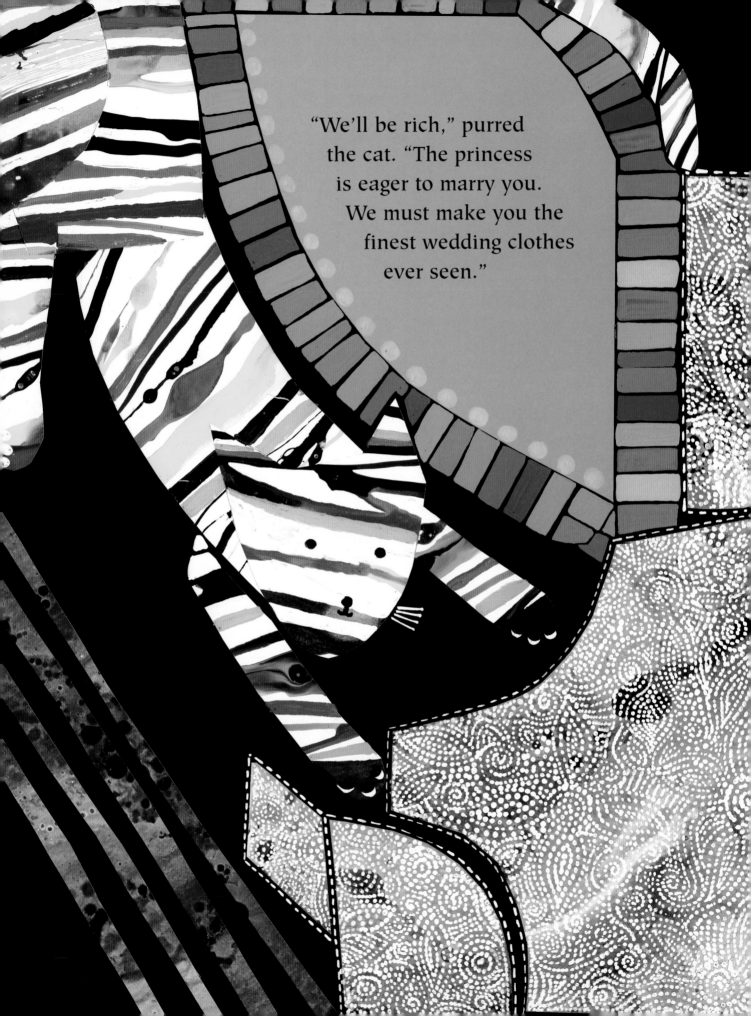

"We'll be rich," purred the cat. "The princess is eager to marry you. We must make you the finest wedding clothes ever seen."

They worked all night and all day and
all the next night and day too.
When Jamil tried on the clothes,
he looked like a prince. Then
Sardul invited some guests
to the wedding...

He went out into the forest and gathered a wild chorus of creatures –

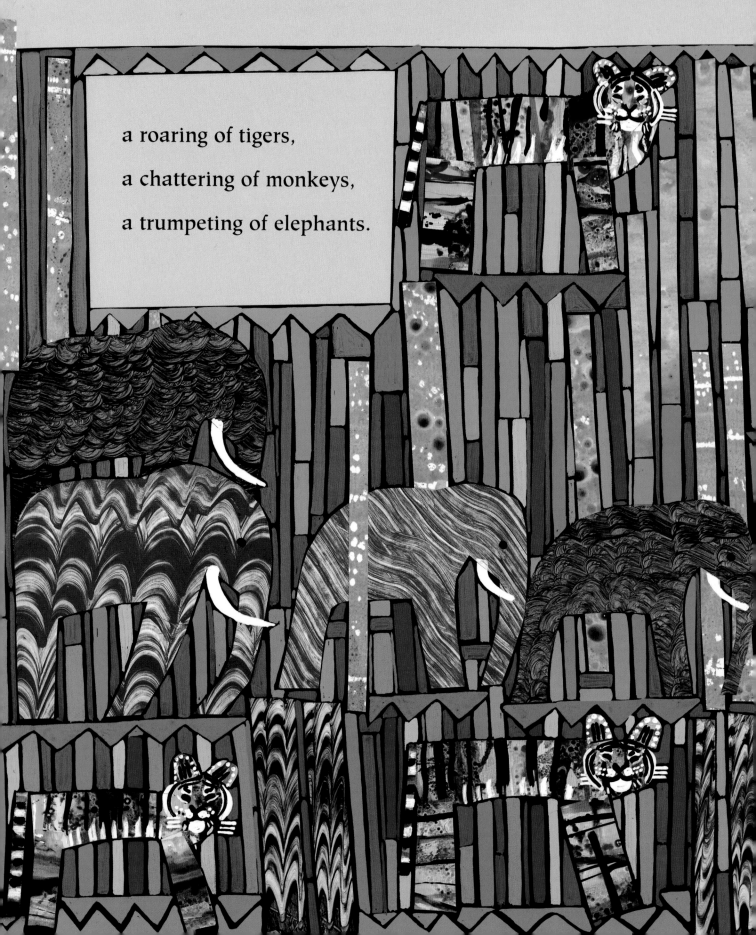

a roaring of tigers,

a chattering of monkeys,

a trumpeting of elephants.

What a noise they made on their way to the palace!

The animals hid among the trees in
the palace garden – and the Rajah
thought the noise was coming from
a thousand people.

"We would be most honoured to meet
the prince," the Rajah said, "but we have
no room for all his retinue."

So Jamil and his cat went into the
palace alone.

Next day, Jamil married the princess.

He looked so rich and handsome – but in truth, he was still Jamil the weaver.

At their wedding feast, he looked up at the ceiling, and said, "What a good place to build a loom. Those beams are just right."

How strange,
thought the princess.
He seems to know
more about weaving
than ruling
a country.

Sardul said quickly,
"We must go. It is
time for my master
to welcome you
to his house."

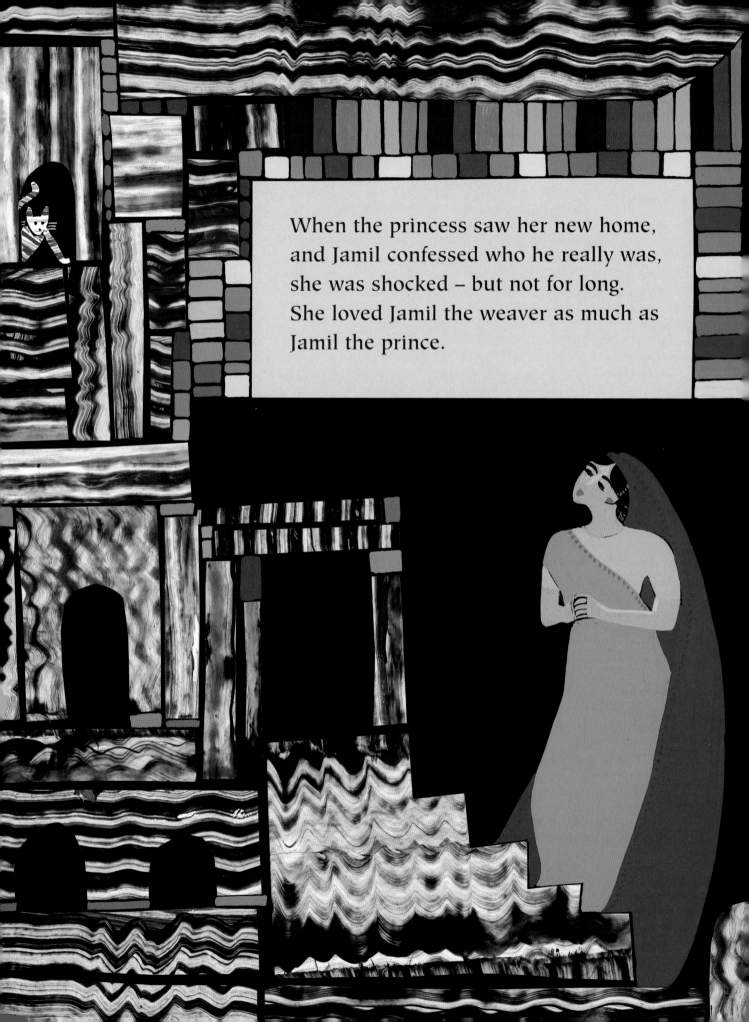

When the princess saw her new home,
and Jamil confessed who he really was,
she was shocked – but not for long.
She loved Jamil the weaver as much as
Jamil the prince.

And so she became a weaver's wife.
She was good at weaving too, after
some practice. At the market, everyone
wanted to buy her beautiful cloth.

Soon she could afford to hire helpers, and she and Jamil became rich. They built a fine new house and other weavers built homes around them. They all worked on the best looms money could buy.

When the Rajah and Ranee came to visit, they found the streets covered in silk, and were met by cheering crowds. Jamil and his wife welcomed them into their home.

"Did I not tell you the truth?" said
Jamil's clever cat. "My master is the
richest man in the world!"